For Max

SIMON & SCHUSTER BOOKS FOR YOUNG READERS
AN IMPRINT OF SIMON & SCHUSTER CHILDREN'S PUBLISHING DIVISION
1230 AVENUE OF THE AMERICAS, NEW YORK, NEW YORK 10020
© 2023 BY JASHAR AWAN
BOOK DESIGN BY LUCY RUTH CUMMINS © 2023 BY SIMON & SCHUSTER, INC.
FOR INFORMATION ABOUT SPECIAL DISCOUNTS FOR BULK PURCHASES, PLEASE CONTACT SIMON & SCHUSTER SPECIAL SALES
AT 1-866-506-1949 OR BUSINESS@SIMONANDSCHUSTER.COM.
THE SIMON & SCHUSTER SPEAKERS BUREAU CAN BRING AUTHORS TO YOUR LIVE EVENT. FOR MORE INFORMATION OR TO
BOOK AN EVENT, CONTACT THE SIMON & SCHUSTER SPEAKERS BUREAU AT 1-866-248-3049 OR VISIT OUR WEBSITE AT
WWW.SIMONSPEAKERS.COM.
THE TEXT FOR THIS BOOK WAS SET IN STRANGE TIMES.
THE ILLUSTRATIONS FOR THIS BOOK WERE RENDERED USING CHARCOAL PENCIL
AND COLORED DIGITALLY WITH ADOBE CREATIVE CLOUD.
MANUFACTURED IN CHINA
0523 SCP
FIRST EDITION
2 4 6 8 10 9 7 5 3 1
CIP DATA FOR THIS BOOK IS AVAILABLE FROM THE LIBRARY OF CONGRESS.
ISBN 9781665938174
ISBN 9781665938181 (EBOOK)

I'm Going to Build a Snowman

BY JASHAR AWAN

SIMON & SCHUSTER BOOKS FOR YOUNG READERS

NEW YORK   LONDON   TORONTO   SYDNEY   NEW DELHI

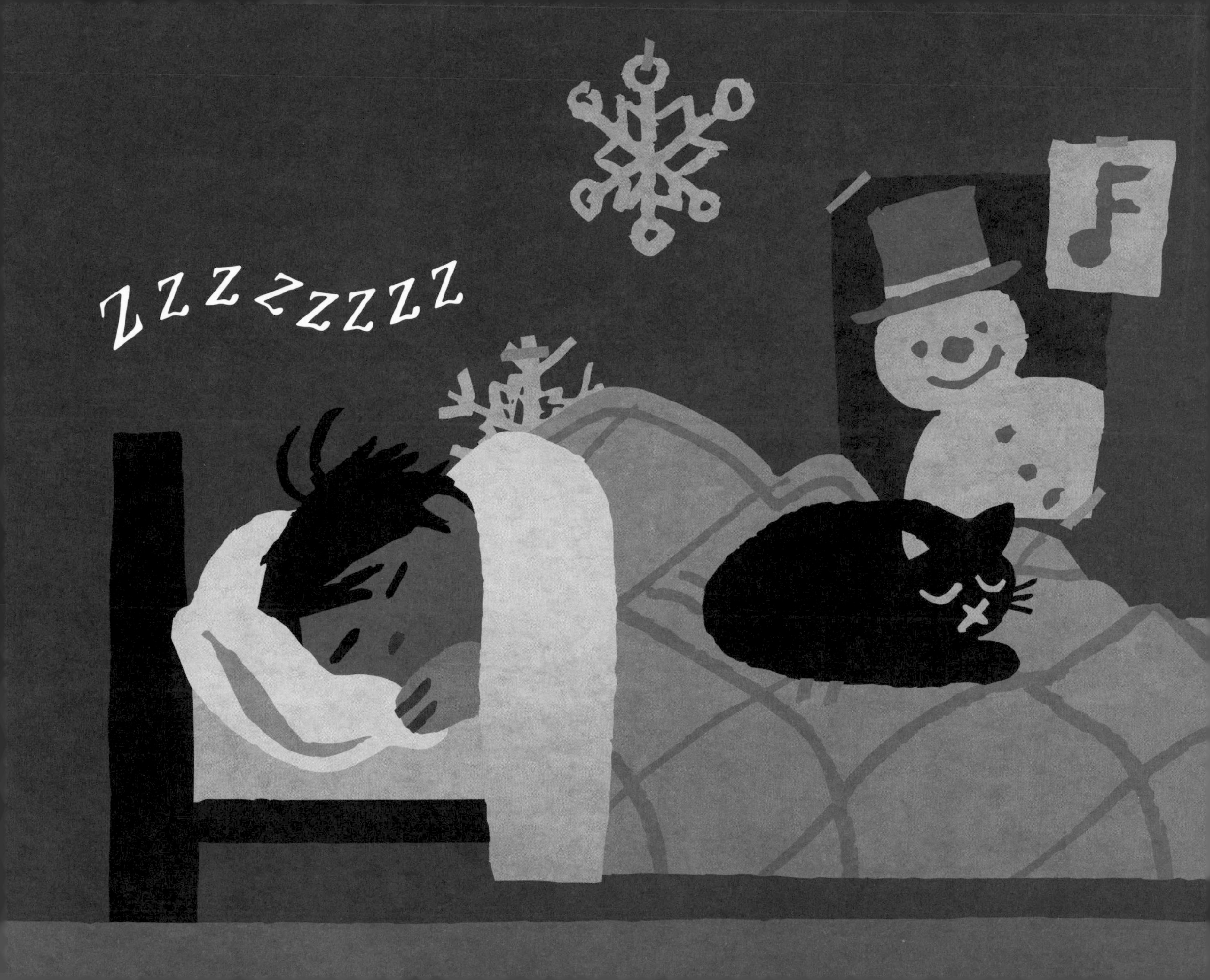
ZZZZZZZZZ

MOM!

It snowed!

You know what that means. . . .

I'm going to build a snowman.

munch
crunch
munch

It'll be
THE BEST SNOWMAN
EVER!

First, gotta put on my sweater and my boots,

and zip up my coat.   Thanks, Mom.

Building a snowman is easy.

Start by rolling
a snowball until
it becomes a
perfect circle.

Next, place a smaller
perfect circle on
top of your previous
perfect circle.

Then, repeat!

Finally, it's time to decorate!
A top hat, a carrot,
and two arm-shaped sticks
will be perfect.

Don't be too surprised when your snowman starts to sing.

And dance . . .

... before you fly off
into the clear night sky.

It will be a dream come true!

If you need me,
I'll be in the yard . . .

building the
BEST SNOWMAN EVER!

All right.

Start with a snowball.

Roll it until

it becomes

a perfect circle.

Time to decorate!

And that's how you build

THE BEST

SNOWMAN EV—

Something's not right. . . .

Sssssslump

Perfect.

HEY, MOM!
TAKE A PICTURE OF ME AND
MY BEST SNOWMAN YET!